Oh, How Silly!

poems selected by
William Cole

drawings by
Tomi Ungerer

Oh, How Silly!

PUFFIN BOOKS

PUFFIN BOOKS   Published by the Penguin Group
Viking Penguin, a division of Penguin Books USA Inc.,
40 West 23rd Street, New York, New York 10010, U.S.A.
Penguin Books Ltd, 27 Wrights Lane, London W8 5TZ, England
Penguin Books Australia Ltd, Ringwood, Victoria, Australia
Penguin Books Canada Ltd, 2801 John Street, Markham, Ontario, Canada L3R 1B4
Penguin Books (N.Z.) Ltd, 182–190 Wairau Road, Auckland 10, New Zealand
Penguin Books Ltd, Registered Offices: Harmondsworth, Middlesex, England

First published in the United States of America by The Viking Press, 1970
Published in Puffin Books, 1990   10 9 8 7 6 5 4 3 2 1
Text copyright © William Cole, 1970   Illustrations copyright © Tomi Ungerer, 1970
All rights reserved

Grateful acknowledgment is made to the following for permission to reprint copyrighted material:
Dennis Dobson, London, for "The ABC" from *The (Little) Pot Boiler* by Spike
Milligan; for "Hello Mr. Python" from *Silly Verse for Kids* by Spike Milligan; and
for "Malice at Buckingham Palace" from *A Book of Bits* by Spike Milligan.
William E. Engel, for "While Grinding Coffee at the Store . . ." and "Willie Built
a Guillotine . . ." Copyright © 1970 by William E. Engel.
Faber and Faber Ltd, for "My Uncle Dan" from *Meet My Folks!* by Ted Hughes.
Farrar, Straus and Giroux, Inc., for "The Crossing of Mary of Scotland," from
Laughing Time by William Jay Smith. Copyright © 1955, 1957, 1980, 1990 by William
Jay Smith. Reprinted by permission of the publisher.
Greenwillow Books, a division of William Morrow and Company, Inc., for "Adelaide"
and "Pigs" by Jack Prelutsky, appearing in his book *The Queen of Eene*. Copyright
© 1970 by Jack Prelutsky.
Mrs. Arthur Guiterman, for "Routine" from *Gaily the Troubador* by Arthur Guiterman.
William Heinemann Ltd., for "Zachary Zed" from *Ragged Robin* by James Reeves.
Copyright © 1961 by James Reeves.
Margaret and Jack Hobbs, Publishers, for "Little Tiny Puppy Dog . . ." from *The
Bedside Milligan* by Spike Milligan.
Alfred A. Knopf, Inc., for "George, Who Played with a Dangerous Toy . . .", "The
Big Baboon," and "The Dodo" from *Cautionary Verses* by Hilaire Belloc. Published
1941 by Alfred A. Knopf, Inc. Reprinted by permission of the publisher.
Little, Brown and Company, for "The Panther," "The Jellyfish," and "The Ostrich"
from *Verses from 1929 On* by Ogden Nash. Copyright 1940, 1942, and 1956 by Ogden Nash.
"The Ostrich" first appeared in *The New Yorker*. By permission of Little, Brown and Company.
Alexander Resnikoff, for "Advice," "Courtship," "Father Goose Tells a Story,"
and "Two Witches." Copyright © 1970 by Alexander Resnikoff.
Shel Silverstein, for "Here Are the Twins . . ." and "Do You Know the Man."
Copyright © 1970 by Shel Silverstein.

LIBRARY OF CONGRESS CATALOGING IN PUBLICATION DATA
Cole, William, 1919–
Oh, how silly : poems / selected by William Cole ; drawings by Tomi Ungerer.   p. cm.
Reprint. Originally published: New York : Viking Press, 1970.
Summary: Fifty-five humorous poems by English and American poets.
ISBN 0-14-034441-1
1. Humorous poetry, American. 2. Children's poetry, American.
3. Humorous poetry, English. 4. Children's poetry, English.
[1. American poetry—Collections. 2. English poetry—Collections.
3. Humorous poetry.] I. Ungerer, Tomi, 1931– , ill. II. Title.
PS595.H803 1990   811'.07089282—dc20   90-30982

Printed in the United States of America   Set in Helvetica

Except in the United States of America, this book is sold subject to the condition that it shall not, by
way of trade or otherwise, be lent, re-sold, hired out, or otherwise circulated without the publisher's
prior consent in any form of binding or cover other than that in which it is published and without a
similar condition including this condition being imposed on the subsequent purchaser.

CONTENTS

Introduction 9
The King Said to Salome, Folk Rhyme 13
Two Sad Tales, Folk Rhyme 14
Here Are the Twins, Shel Silverstein 15
Politeness, Harry Graham 16
Courtship, Alexander Resnikoff 18
Deborah Delora, English Folk Rhyme 19
The ABC, Spike Milligan 20
The Sea Serpent: An Accurate Description, Wallace Irwin 22
Malice at Buckingham Palace, Spike Milligan 24
The Jellyfish, Ogden Nash 25
Ten Thousand Years Ago, American Nonsense Song 26
Pigs, Jack Prelutsky 27
The Big Baboon, Hilaire Belloc 28
The Ostrich, Ogden Nash 28
A Llyric of the Llama, Burges Johnson 30
Little Tiny Puppy Dog, Spike Milligan 31

Two Witches, Alexander Resnikoff   33
Zachary Zed, James Reeves   34
Framed in a First-story Winder . . . , Anonymous   36
Silly Stanzas, American Folk Rhymes   38
George, Hilaire Belloc   40
Willie Built a Guillotine, William E. Engel   43
The Puffin, Robert Williams Wood   44
Two Legs Behind and Two Before, Folk Rhyme   45
Gentle Doctor Brown, Bert Leston Taylor   46
The Panther, Ogden Nash   48
Hello Mr. Python, Spike Milligan   48
My Uncle Dan, Ted Hughes   50
Hannah Bantry, Nursery Rhyme   52
While Grinding Coffee at the Store, William E. Engel   53
The Boy Stood on the Burning Deck (two versions), American Folk Rhymes   54
Adelaide, Jack Prelutsky   56
Advice to Grandsons, Anonymous   58
Dumbbell, William Cole   59
Father Goose Tells a Story, Alexander Resnikoff   60
As I Was Standing in the Street, American Folk Rhyme   62
The Cumberbunce, Paul West   63
The Dodo, Hilaire Belloc   68
Glue, Gelett Burgess   69
Routine, Arthur Guiterman   70
Rhinoceroses, Anonymous   71
Johnny Went to Church One Day, American Folk Rhymes   72

The Lady and the Swine, English Folk Rhyme   74
The Crossing of Mary of Scotland, William Jay Smith   75
Do You Know the Man?, Shel Silverstein   76
Who Ever Sausage a Thing?, Anonymous   77
The Horses Run Around, American Nonsense Song   78
Fascination, John Bannister Tabb   80
Learner, English Children's Rhyme   81
Old Joe Clarke, American Folk Song   82
The Lazy People, Shel Silverstein   83
Advice, Alexander Resnikoff   84
Some Sights Sometimes Seen and Seldom Seen, William Cole   85
East Is East and West Is West, Sign in a Ceylon Zoo   86
The Big Rock Candy Mountain, American Folk Song   87
  Author Index   91
  Title Index   93

INTRODUCTION

This
skin-
ny
poem
will
in-
tro-
duce

This
sil-
ly
book
which
has
no
use

Ex-
cept,
I
hope,
to
make
you
grin

(My
good-
ness,

but
this
poem
is
thin!)

If
you
should
like
this
sil-
ly
stuff

And
find
you
can-
not
get
e-
nough

Just
go
in-
to
your
li-
brar-
y

And
ask
for
oth-
er
books
by
me.

(And
Tom-
i
Ung-
er-
er
al-
so

Has
fun-
ny-
books
to
make
you
glow.)

I
hope
this
stuff
a-

**mus-
es
you;**

**Good-
bye,
fare-
well,
and
too-
dle-
oo.**

William Cole

Oh, How Silly!

THE KING SAID TO SALOME

The King said to Salome,
"We'll have no dancing here!"
Salome said, "The heck with you!"
And kicked the chandelier.

Folk rhyme

TWO SAD TALES

Smarty, Smarty,
Gave a party—
Nobody came.

Smarty, Smarty,
Gave another party—
Just the same.

Folk rhyme

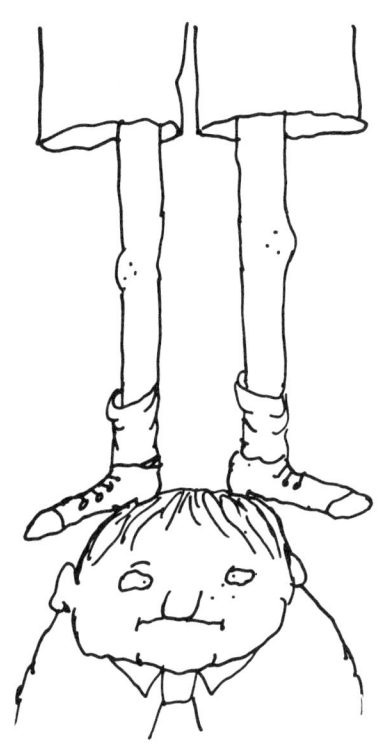

Here are the twins,
Dan and Stan.
Each one is a
Different sort.
For Dan is too tall
to fit on
the page,
and Stan
is a little
too short.

Shel Silverstein

POLITENESS

My cousin John was most polite;
   He led shortsighted Mrs. Bond,
By accident, one winter's night
   Into a village pond.
Her life perhaps he might have saved
But how genteelly he behaved!

Each time she rose and waved to him
   He smiled and bowed and doffed his hat;
Thought he, although I cannot swim,
   At least I can do that—
And when for the third time she sank
He stood bareheaded on the bank.

Be civil, then, to young and old;
   Especially to persons who
Possess a quantity of gold
   Which they might leave to you.
The more they have, it seems to me,
The more polite you ought to be.

Harry Graham

COURTSHIP

Said a porcupine:
"Dear Miss Pin Cushine,
It's for you I pine;
I wish you were mine. . . .

Will you be my Valentine?"

Said Miss Pin Cushion:
"My dear Porcupin,
It's really a sin
But me you cannot win—

IF YOU DON'T KNOW THE DIFFERENCE
Between PINE and PIN!"

Alexander Resnikoff

DEBORAH DELORA

Deborah Delora, she liked a bit of fun—
She went to the baker's and she bought a penny bun;
Dipped the bun in treacle and threw it at her teacher—
Deborah Delora! what a wicked creature!

English folk rhyme

THE ABC

'Twas midnight in the schoolroom
And every desk was shut,
When suddenly from the alphabet
Was heard a loud "Tut-tut!"

Said A to B, "I don't like C;
His manners are a lack.
For all I ever see of C
Is a semicircular back!"

"I disagree," said D to B,
"I've never found C so.
From where *I* stand, he seems to be
An uncompleted O."

C was vexed, "I'm much perplexed,
You criticize my shape.
I'm made like that, to help spell Cat
And Cow and Cool and Cape."

"He's right," said E; said F, "Whoopee!"
Said G, " 'Ip, 'ip, 'ooray!"
"You're dropping me," roared H to G.
"Don't do it please, I pray!"

"Out of my way," LL said to K.
"I'll make poor I look ILL."
To stop this stunt, J stood in front,
And presto! ILL was JILL.

"U know," said V, "that W
Is twice the age of me,
For as a Roman V is five
I'm half as young as he."

X and Y yawned sleepily,
"Look at the time!" they said.
They all jumped in to beddy byes
And the last one in was Z!

Spike Milligan

THE SEA SERPANT

An Accurate Description

A-sleepin' at length on the sand,
    Where the beach was all tidy and clean,
A-strokin' his scale with the brush on his tail
    The wily Sea Serpant I seen.

And what was his colour? you asks,
    And how did he look? inquires you,
I'll be busted and blessed if he didn't look jest
    Like you would of expected 'im to!

His head was the size of a—well,
    The size what they always attains;
He whistled a tune what was built like a prune,
    And his tail was the shape o' his brains.

His scales they was ruther—you know—
    Like the leaves what you pick off o' eggs;
And the way o' his walk—well, it's useless to talk,
    Fer o' course you've seen Sea Serpants' legs.

His length it was seventeen miles,
    Or fathoms, or inches, or feet
(Me memory's sich that I can't recall which,
    Though at figgers I've seldom been beat).

And I says as I looks at the beast,
    "He reminds me o' somethin' I've seen—

Is it candy or cats or humans or hats,
  Or Fenimore Cooper I mean?"

And as I debated the point,
  In a way that I can't understand,
The Sea Serpant he disappeared in the sea
  And walked through the ocean by land.

And somehow I knowed he'd come back,
  So I marked off the place with me cap;
'Twas Latitude West and Longitude North
  And forty-eight cents by the map.

And his length it was seventeen miles,
  Or inches, or fathoms, or feet
(Me memory's sich that I can't recall which,
  Though at figgers I've seldom been beat).

Wallace Irwin

MALICE AT BUCKINGHAM PALACE

Outside Buckingham Palace
  a dog was barking one day
When out of a house
  came a chocolate mouse
And frightened that doggie away.

And so that chocolate mousie
  was taken to the Queen—
Who swallowed him up
  with a gobbledy glup.
I do think that was mean.

Spike Milligan

THE JELLYFISH

Who wants my jellyfish?
I'm not sellyfish!

Ogden Nash

TEN THOUSAND YEARS AGO

I was born about ten thousand years ago,
And there's nothing in this world I do not know;
   I saw Balaam on his mule
   Ridin' off to Sunday school,
And I'll lick the guy who says it isn't so.

I taught Solomon his little A-B-C's,
I was there when they first made Limburger cheese;
   I was sailing down the bay,
   With Methuselah one day,
And I saw his whiskers waving in the breeze.

Queen Elizabeth she fell in love with me,
We were married in Milwaukee secretly;
   I was in an airplane flying
   When George Washington stopped lying,
And I once held Cleopatra on my knee.

I was there when Satan looked the garden o'er,
I saw Eve and Adam driven from the door;
   I was behind the bushes peekin'
   At the apple they was eatin'
And I swear that I'm the guy who ate the core.

American nonsense song

PIGS

Pigs are stout
and pigs are kind
and pigs are seldom clean.

snout before
and tail behind
and bacon in between

Jack Prelutsky

THE BIG BABOON

The Big Baboon is found upon
    The Plains of Cariboo:
He goes about with nothing on
    (A shocking thing to do).

But if he dressed respectably
    And let his whiskers grow,
How like this Big Baboon would be
    To Mister So-and-So!

Hilaire Belloc

THE OSTRICH

The ostrich roams the great Sahara.
Its mouth is wide, its neck is narra.
It has such long and lofty legs,
I'm glad it sits to lay its eggs.

Ogden Nash

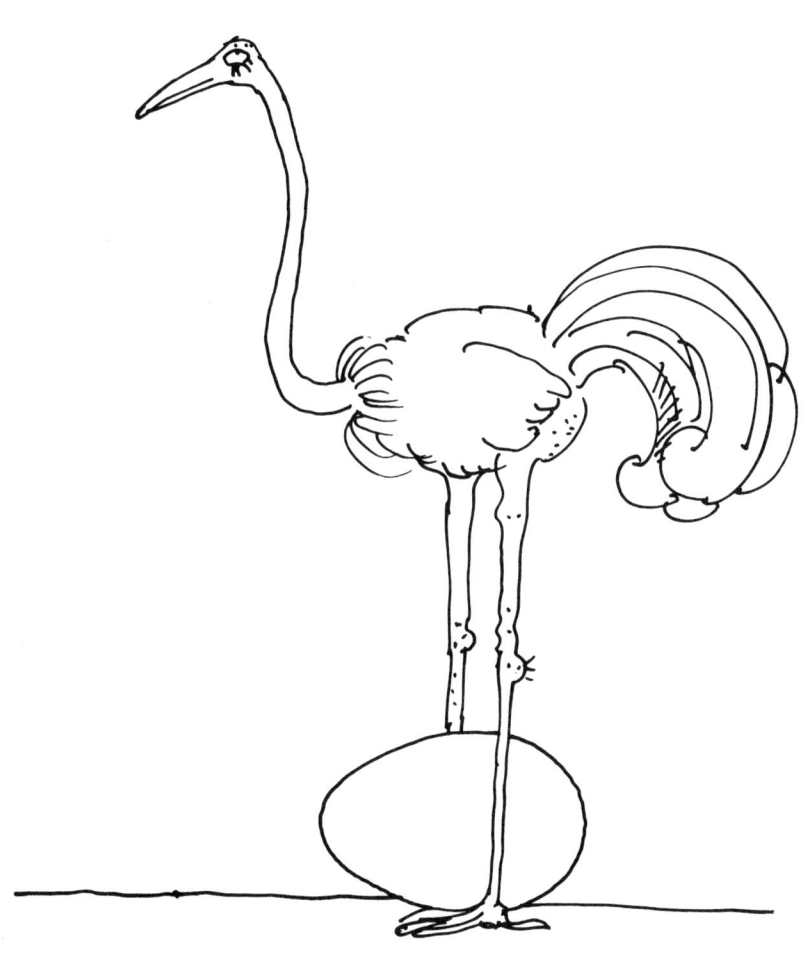

A LLYRIC OF THE LLAMA

Behold how from her lair the youthful llama
    Llopes forth and llightly scans the llandscape o'er.
With llusty heart she llooks upon llife's drama,
    Relying on her llate-llearnt worldly llore.

But llo! Some llad, armed with a yoke *infama*,
    Soon llures her into llowly llabor's cause;
Her wool is llopped to weave into pajama,
    And llanguidly she llearns her Gees and Haws.

My children, heed this llesson from all llanguishing young
   lllamas,
   If you would lllive with lllatitude, avoid each llluring
      lllay;
And do not lllightly lllleave, I beg, your llllonesome,
   lllloving mammas,
   And llllast of alllll, don't spelllll your name in such a
      sillllllly way.

Burges Johnson

Little tiny puppy dog
Sleeping soundly as a log
Better wake him for his dinner
Or else he'll start to sleep much thinner.

Spike Milligan

TWO WITCHES

There was a witch
The witch had an itch
The itch was so itchy it
Gave her a twitch.

Another witch
Admired the twitch
So she started twitching
Though she had no itch.

Now both of them twitch
So it's hard to tell which
Witch has the itch and
Which witch has the twitch.

Alexander Resnikoff

ZACHARY ZED

Zachary Zed was the last man,
    The last man left on earth.
For everyone else had died but him
    And no more come to birth.

In former times young Zachary
    Had asked a maid to wed.
"I loves thee, dear," he told her true,
    "Will thou be Missis Zed?"

"No, not if you was the last man
    On earth!" the maid replied;
And he was; but she wouldn't give consent,
    And in due time she died.

So all alone stood Zachary.
  " 'Tis not so bad," he said,
"There's no one to make me brush my hair
  Nor send me up to bed.

"There's none can call me wicked,
  Nor none to argufy,
So dang my soul if I don't per-nounce
  LONG LIVE KING ZACHAR-Y!"

So Zachary Zed was the last man
  And the last King beside,
And never a person lived to tell
  If ever Zachary died.

James Reeves

FRAMED IN
A FIRST-STORY
WINDER

Framed in a first-story winder of a burnin' buildin'
Appeared: A Yuman Ead!
Jump into this net, wot we are 'oldin'
And yule be quite orl right!

But 'ee wouldn't jump . . .

And the flames grew Igher and Igher and Igher.
(Phew!)

Framed in a second-story winder of a burnin' buildin'
Appeared: A Yuman Ead!
Jump into this net, wot we are 'oldin'
And yule be quite orl right!

But 'ee wouldn't jump . . .

And the flames grew Igher and Igher and Igher
(Strewth!)

Framed in a third-story winder of a burnin' buildin'
Appeared: A Yuman Ead!
Jump into this net, wot we are 'oldin'
And yule be quite orl right!
Honest!

And 'ee jumped . . .

And 'ee broke 'is bloomin' neck!

Anonymous

SILLY STANZAS

A peanut sat on a railroad track,
His heart was all a-flutter;
The five-fifteen came rushing by—
Toot! toot! peanut butter!

A froggie sat on a lily pad
Looking up at the sky;
The lily pad broke and the frog fell in,
Water all in his eye.

A man he lived by the sewer
And by the sewer he died,
And at the coroner's inquest
They called it sewer-side.

A rabbit raced a turtle,
You know the turtle won;
And Mister Bunny came in late,
A little hot cross bun!

American folk rhymes

GEORGE

*Who played with a dangerous toy,
and suffered a catastrophe of
Considerable dimensions*

When George's Grandmamma was told
That George had been as good as Gold,
She promised in the Afternoon
To buy him an *Immense* BALLOON.

And so she did; but when it came,
It got into the candle flame,
And being of a dangerous sort
Exploded with a loud report!
The Lights went out! The Windows Broke!

The Room was filled with reeking smoke,
And in the darkness shrieks and yells
Were mingled with Electric Bells,
And falling masonry and groans,
And crunching, as of broken bones,
And dreadful shrieks, when, worst of all,
The House itself began to fall!
It tottered, shuddering to and fro,
Then crashed into the street below—
Which happened to be Savile Row.

When Help arrived, among the Dead
Were Cousin Mary, Little Fred,
The Footmen (both of them), the Groom,
The man that cleaned the Billiard-Room,
The Chaplain, and the Still-Room Maid.

And I am dreadfully afraid
That Monsieur Champignon, the Chef,
Will now be permanently deaf—
And both his Aides are much the same;
While George, who was in part to blame,
Received, you will regret to hear,
A nasty lump behind the ear.

Moral

The moral is that little Boys
Should not be given dangerous Toys.

Hilaire Belloc

WILLIE BUILT A GUILLOTINE

Willie built a guillotine,
Tried it out on sister Jean.
Said Mother as she got the mop:
"These messy games have got to stop!"

William E. Engel

THE PUFFIN

Upon this cake of ice is perched
The paddle-footed Puffin;
To find his double we have searched,
But have discovered— Nuffin!

Robert Williams Wood

TWO LEGS BEHIND AND TWO BEFORE

(To be sung to the tune of "Auld Lang Syne")

On mules we find two legs behind,
    And two we find before;
We stand behind before we find
    What the two behind be for.
When we're behind the two behind,
    We find what these be for;
So stand before the two behind,
    And behind the two before.

Folk rhyme

GENTLE DOCTOR BROWN

It was a gentle sawbones and his name was Doctor Brown.
His auto was the terror of a small suburban town.
His practice, quite amazing for so trivial a place,
Consisted of the victims of his homicidal pace.

So constant was his practice and so high his motor's gear
That at knocking down pedestrians he never had a peer;
But it must, in simple justice, be as truly written down

That no man could be more thoughtful than gentle Doctor
  Brown.

Whatever was the errand on which Doctor Brown was bent
He'd stop to patch a victim up and never charged a cent.
He'd always pause, whoever 'twas he happened to run down:
A humane and a thoughtful man was gentle Doctor Brown.

"How fortunate," he would observe, "how fortunate 'twas I
That knocked you galley-west and heard your wild and
  wailing cry.
There *are* some heartless wretches who would leave you here
  alone,
Without a sympathetic ear to catch your dying moan.

"Such callousness," said Doctor Brown, "I cannot comprehend;
To fathom such indifference I simply don't pretend.
One ought to do his duty, and I never am remiss.
A simple word of thanks is all I ask. Here, swallow this!"

Then, reaching in the tonneau, he'd unpack his little kit,
And perform an operation that was workmanlike and fit.
"You may survive," said Doctor Brown; "it's happened
  once or twice.
If not, you've had the benefit of competent advice."

Oh, if all our motormaniacs were equally humane,
How little bitterness there'd be, or reason to complain!
How different our point of view if we were ridden down
By lunatics as thoughtful as gentle Doctor Brown!

Bert Leston Taylor

THE PANTHER

The panther is like a leopard,
Except it hasn't been peppered.
Should you behold a panther crouch,
Prepare to say Ouch.
Better yet, if called by a panther,
Don't anther.

Ogden Nash

HELLO MR. PYTHON

Hello Mr. Python
Curling round a tree,
Bet you'd like to make yourself
A dinner out of me.

Can't you change your habits
Crushing people's bones?
I wouldn't like a dinner
That emitted fearful groans.

Spike Milligan

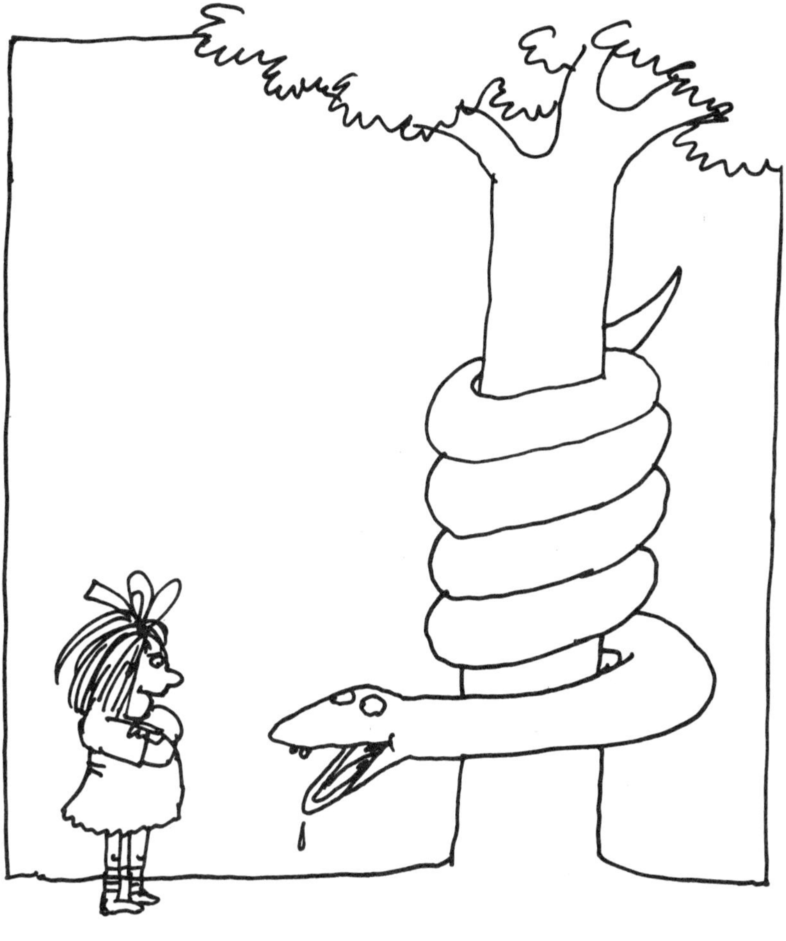

MY UNCLE DAN

My Uncle Dan's an inventor, you may think that's very fine.
You may wish he was your Uncle instead of being mine—
If he wanted he could make a watch that bounces when it drops,
He could make a helicopter out of string and bottle tops
Or any really useful thing you can't get in the shops.
    But Uncle Dan has other ideas:
    The bottomless glass for ginger beers,
    The toothless saw that's safe for the tree,
    A special word for a spelling bee

(Like Lionocerangoutangadder),
Or the roll-uppable rubber ladder,
The mystery pie that bites when it's bit—
My Uncle Dan invented it.
My Uncle Dan sits in his den inventing night and day.
His eyes peer from his hair and beard like mice from a load of hay.
And does he make the shoes that will go walks without your feet?
A shrinker to shrink instantly the elephants you meet?
A carver that just carves from the air steaks cooked and ready to eat?
No, no, he has other intentions—
Only perfectly useless inventions:
Glassless windows (they never break),
A medicine to cure the earthquake,
The unspillable screwed-down cup,
The stairs that go neither down nor up,
The door you simply paint on a wall—
Uncle Dan invented them all.

Ted Hughes

Hannah Bantry, in the pantry,
Gnawing a mutton bone;
How she gnawed it!
How she clawed it!
When she found herself alone.

Nursery rhyme

While grinding coffee at the store
Will disappeared, was seen no more.
Said Pa, who's handy with a quip,
"I hope that it was set for drip."

William E. Engel

THE BOY STOOD ON THE BURNING DECK

The boy stood on the burning deck
Eating peanuts by the peck;
His father called him, he wouldn't go,
Because he loved the peanuts so.

AND . . .

The boy stood on the burning deck,
His feet were full of blisters;
The flames came up and burned his pants,
And now he wears his sister's.

American folk rhymes

ADELAIDE

Adelaide was quite dismayed;
the more she ate, the less she weighed;
the less she weighed, the more she ate,
and addled Adelaide lost weight.

She stuffed herself with meat and cheese,
potatoes, pumpkins, pies and peas,
but standing on the scale she found
that she had shed at least a pound.

She gorged herself on breasts of veal,
on roasted fish, on pickled eel,
but on completion of this feast
her scale read—ten pounds less, at least.

Poor Adelaide, that foolish glutton,
filled herself with heaps of mutton,
but when this was finally done
the scale said—minus twenty-one.

She ate until her face turned blue—
she did not know what else to do—
but when she'd finished with her plate,
she'd lost a hundred pounds of weight.

Soon Adelaide, by all accounts,
was down to hardly half an ounce,
and yet what filled her with despair
was that her cupboard shelves were bare.

For Adelaide still wished to eat—
then spied a bread crumb by her feet;
she swiftly plucked it off the floor,
and swallowed it, then was— no more!

Jack Prelutsky

ADVICE TO GRANDSONS

When grandma visits you, my dears,
   Be good as you can be;
Don't put hot waffles in her ears,
   Or beetles in her tea.

Don't sew a pattern on her cheek
   With worsted or with silk;
Don't call her naughty names in Greek,
   Or spray her face with milk.

Don't drive a staple in her foot,
   Don't stick pins in her head;
And, oh, I beg you, do not put
   Live embers in her bed.

These things are not considered kind;
    They worry her, and tease—
Such cruelty is not refined
    It always fails to please.

Be good to grandma, little chaps,
    Whatever else you do;
And then she'll grow to be—perhaps—
    More tolerant of you.

Anonymous

DUMBBELL

My teacher is mad; he wants to know,
But I *can't* Remember the Alamo!

William Cole

FATHER GOOSE TELLS A STORY

Ah! Good evening, my dear!
I wonder, did you ever hear
The story of the bear and the deer?

Well, there once was this little deer
And one day he met with a beer—
Of course I do not mean beer
I got it mixed up I fear
I'll start all over, you hear?
I *didn't* ask if you're here
I *know* that you are here, my dear
But I was telling you about that deer
Who met no beer but a *bear*.

THERE!

What? What do you mean by "*where*"?
I just said "*there*" to say "*there*"
I didn't mean *any*where!
Don't interrupt, that isn't fair
Interruptions I cannot bear....
As I was saying, this bear,
One day he met with a dare—
I mean a deer, now look here, my dear
You want to hear about this deer
Or don't you want to hear?

So there was a deer, *any*where
Who one day met with a bear
And the *deer* said to the *bear:*
"What's all this noise that I hair?"
Oh come come, my dear! Of course I mean "hear"!
WHAT ARE YOU COMING FOR HERE?!
I did NOT say to come HERE!
Oh, c'mon now, can't you hear?
Now about that There and the Here—
Oh dear, oh dear, oh my dear
I can't even STAND that deer!
I can't even BEAR that bear!!
WHAT?! Same to you! So there!

Alexander Resnikoff

AS I WAS STANDING IN THE STREET

> As I was standing in the street,
>   As quiet as could be,
> A great big ugly man came up
>   And tied his horse to me.

American folk rhyme

THE CUMBERBUNCE

I strolled beside the shining sea,
I was as lonely as could be;
No one to cheer me in my walk
But stones and sand, which cannot talk—
Sand and stones and bits of shell,
Which never have a thing to tell.

But as I sauntered by the tide
I saw a something at my side,
A something green, and blue, and pink,
And brown, and purple, too, I think.
I would not say how large it was;
I would not venture that, because
It took me rather by surprise,
And I have not the best of eyes.

Should you compare it to a cat,
I'd say it was as large as that;
Or should you ask me if the thing
Was smaller than a sparrow's wing,
I should be apt to think you knew,
And simply answer, "Very true!"
Well, as I looked upon the thing,
It murmured, "Please, sir, can I sing?"
And then I knew its name at once—
It plainly was a Cumberbunce.

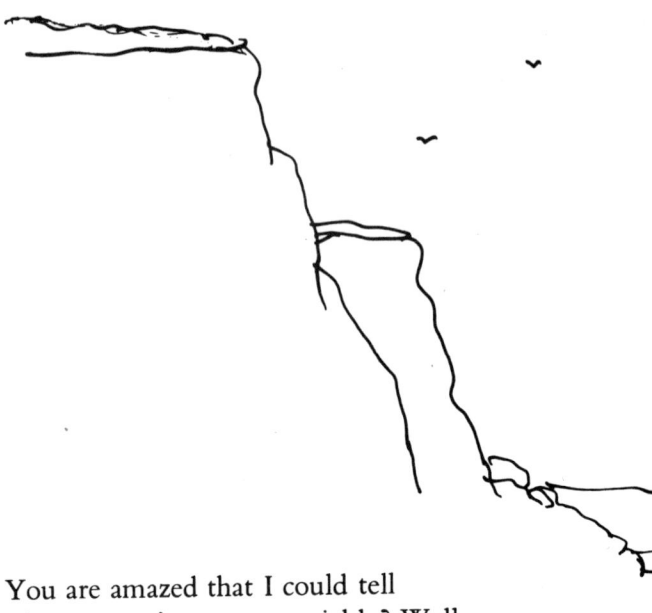

You are amazed that I could tell
The creature's name so quickly? Well,
I knew it was not a paper doll,
A pencil or a parasol,
A tennis racket or a cheese,
And, as it was not one of these,
And I am not a perfect dunce—
It had to be a Cumberbunce!

With pleading voice and tearful eye
It seemed as though about to cry.
It looked so pitiful and sad
It made me feel extremely bad.
My heart was softened to the thing
That asked me if it, please, could sing.

Its little hand I longed to shake,
But, oh, it had no hand to take!
I bent and drew the creature near,
And whispered in its pale-blue ear,
"What! Sing, my Cumberbunce? You can!
Sing on, sing loudly, little man!"

The Cumberbunce, without ado,
Gazed sadly on the ocean blue,
And, lifting up its little head,
In tones of awful longing, said:

"Oh, I would sing of mackerel skies,
  And why the sea is wet,
Of jellyfish and conger eels,
  And things that I forget.
And I would hum a plaintive tune
  Of why the waves are hot
As water boiling on a stove,
  Excepting that they're not!

"And I would sing of hooks and eyes,
  And why the sea is slant,
And gaily tips the little ships,
  Excepting that I can't!
I never sang a single song,
  I never hummed a note.
There is in me no melody,
  No music in my throat.

"So that is why I do not sing
Of sharks, or whales, or anything!"

I looked in innocent surprise,
My wonder showing in my eyes.
"Then why, O Cumberbunce," I cried,
"Did you come walking at my side
And ask me if you, please, might sing,
When you could not warble anything?"

"I did not ask permission, sir,
I really did not, I aver.
You, sir, misunderstood me, quite.
I did not ask you if I *might*.
Had you correctly understood,
You'd know I asked you if I *could*
So, as I cannot sing a song,
Your answer, it is plain, was wrong.
The fact I could not sing I knew,
But wanted your opinion, too."

A voice came softly o'er the lea.
   "Farewell! my mate is calling me!"
I saw the creature disappear,
Its voice, in parting, smote my ear—
"I thought all people understood
The difference 'twixt 'might' and 'could'!"

Paul West

THE DODO

The Dodo used to walk around,
   And take the sun and air.
The sun yet warms his native ground—
   The Dodo is not there!

The voice which used to squawk and squeak
   Is now forever dumb—
Yet may you see his bones and beak
   All in the Mu-se-um.

Hilaire Belloc

GLUE

If the streets were filled with glue,
What d'you s'pose you would do?
If you should go to walk at night,
In the morning you'd be stuck tight!

Gelett Burgess

ROUTINE

No matter what we are and who,
Some duties everyone must do:

A Poet puts aside his wreath
To wash his face and brush his teeth,

And even Earls
Must comb their curls,

And even Kings
Have underthings.

Arthur Guiterman

RHINOCEROSES

No one for spelling at a loss is
Who boldly spells Rhinocerosses;
I've known a few (I can't say lots)
Who call the beasts Rhinocerots,
Though they are not so bad, say I,
As those who say Rhinoceri.
One I have heard (O holy Moses!)
Who plainly said Rhinoceroses,
Another one—a brilliant boy—
Insists that it's Rhinoceroi—
The moral that I draw from these is
The plural's what one darn well pleases.

Anonymous

JOHNNY WENT TO CHURCH ONE DAY

Johnny went to church one day,
He climbed up on the steeple;
He took his shoes and stockings off
And threw them at the people.

Johnny stole a penny once,
And to the court was sent;
The judge found Johnny guilty,
But he was in a cent.

The firefly is a funny bug,
He hasn't any mind;
He blunders all the way through life
With his headlight on behind.

The skeeter likes a hairless man,
With him he's quite at home;
No better pasture can he find
Than on a bald man's dome.

Some people say that fleas are black,
But I know it isn't so;
For Mary had a little lamb
Whose fleas was white as snow.

There's a cross-eyed woman in our town,
She's cross-eyed, that's a fact;
And every time the lady cries,
The tears roll down her back.

American folk rhymes

THE LADY AND THE SWINE

There was a lady loved a swine;
  "Honey," said she,
"Pig-hog, wilt thou be mine?"
  "Oink," said he.

"I'll build for thee a silver sty,
 Honey," said she,
"And in it softly thou shalt lie."
 "Oink," said he.

"Pinned with a silver pin,
 Honey," said she,
"That you may go both out and in."
 "Oink," said he.

"When shall we two be wed,
 Honey?" said she.
"Oink, oink, oink," he said,
 And away went he.

English folk rhyme

THE CROSSING OF MARY OF SCOTLAND

Mary, Mary, Queen of Scots,
Dressed in yellow polka dots,
Sailed one rainy winter day,
Sailed from Dover to Calais,
Sailed in tears, heart tied in knots;
Face broke out in scarlet spots
The size of yellow polka dots—
Forgot to take her *booster* shots,
Queen of Scotland, Queen of Scots!

William Jay Smith

DO YOU KNOW THE MAN?

Do you know the man with the flowers growing
Out of the top of his head?
Yellow flowers,
Purple flowers,
Orange, green, and red.
Growing there
Just like hair
Out of the top of his head.
(Yes, you heard just what I said—
Out of the top of his head.)

Shel Silverstein

WHO EVER SAUSAGE A THING?

One day a boy went walking
And went into a store;
He bought a pound of sausages
And laid them on the floor.

The boy began to whistle
A merry little tune—
And all the little sausages
Danced around the room!

Anonymous

THE HORSES RUN AROUND

The horses run around,
Their feet are on the ground,
O who will wind the clocks when I'm away? (away)
Go get the axe,
There's a hair on Baby's chin,
And a man's best friend is his mother. (no other)

While looking out a window,
A second-story window,
I slipped and sprained my eyebrow on the pavement; (the pavement)
Go get the Listerine,
Sister's got a beau,
And who cut the sleeves off Father's vest? (his vest)

I was looking through a knothole
In Father's wooden leg—
Why did they put the shore so near the ocean? (the ocean)
We feed the baby garlic
So we'll find him in the dark,
And the monkeys have no tails in Zamboanga! (Boanga)

American nonsense song

FASCINATION

Among your many playmates here,
How is it that you all prefer
   Your little friend, my dear?
"Because, mamma, though hard we try,
Not one of us can spit so high,
   And catch it in his ear."

John Bannister Tabb

LEARNER

Oh, Matilda, look at your Uncle Jim,
He's in the bathtub learning how to swim.
First he does the front stroke, then he does the side,
Now he's underwater swimming against the tide.

English children's rhyme

OLD JOE CLARKE

Old Joe Clarke, he had a house,
Was fifteen stories high,
And every darn room in that house
Was full of chicken pie.

I went down to Old Joe Clarke's
And found him eating supper;
I stubbed my toe on the table leg
And stuck my nose in the butter.

I went down to Old Joe Clarke's
But Old Joe wasn't in;
I sat right down on the red-hot stove
And got right up again.

Old Joe Clarke had a candy box
To keep his sweetheart in;
He'd take her out and kiss her twice
And put her back again.

American folk song

THE LAZY PEOPLE

Let's write a poem about lazy people
Who lazily laze their lives away;
Let's finish it tomorrow,
I'm much too tired today.

Shel Silverstein

ADVICE

Here's a nice advice:
If your mice have lice,
Rub them with a slice of ice
And sprinkle them with spice.
(Do this every morning once—
And in the evening twice.)

Alexander Resnikoff

SOME SIGHTS
SOMETIMES SEEN
AND SELDOM SEEN

You don't have to go very far
To see a boat towed by a car;
But to see a car towed by a boat
Is *really* a matter of note.

To see a truck pulling a horse
In a van is a matter of course;
But to see a horse pulling a truck
In a van is *extremely* good luck.

William Cole

EAST IS EAST AND WEST IS WEST

East is East and West is West,
Though this may not seem relevant.
We all know how to milk a cow,
But you can't muck about with an elephant.

Sign in a Ceylon Zoo

THE BIG ROCK CANDY MOUNTAIN

On a summer's day in the month of May
A burly bum come a-hikin'
Down a shady lane through the sugar cane;
He was lookin' for his likin'.
As he roamed along he sang a song
'Bout a land of milk and honey,
Where a bum can stay for many a day
And he won't need any money.
  Oh, the buzzin' of the bees in the cigarette trees,
  The soda-water fountain;
  The lemonade springs where the bluebird sings,
  In the big rock candy mountain!

In the big rock candy mountain
All the cops have wooden legs,
And the bulldogs all have rubber teeth,
And the hens lay hard-boiled eggs;
The farmers' trees are full of fruit,
The barns are full of hay;
Oh, I'm bound to go where there ain't no snow,
Where the rain don't fall and the wind don't blow,
In the big rock candy mountain.
Oh, the buzzin' of the bees . . .

In the big rock candy mountain
You never change your socks;
And the little streams of alkyhol
Come a-tricklin' down the rocks;
The jails they all are made of tin,
The railroad bulls are blind;
There's a lake of stew, and whisky too,
You can paddle all around in a big canoe,
In the big rock candy mountain.
  Oh, the buzzin' of the bees . . .

American folk song

AUTHOR INDEX

Belloc, Hilaire, *Big Baboon, The*   28
  Dodo, The   68
  George   40
Burgess, Gelett, *Glue*   69
Cole, William, *Dumbbell*   59
  Some Sights Sometimes Seen and Seldom Seen   85
Engel, William E., *While Grinding Coffee at the Store*   53
  Willie Built a Guillotine   43
Graham, Harry, *Politeness*   16
Guiterman, Arthur, *Routine*   70
Hughes, Ted, *My Uncle Dan*   50
Irwin, Wallace, *The Sea Serpant: An Accurate Description*   22
Johnson, Burges, *A Llyric of the Llama*   30
Milligan, Spike, *ABC, The*   20
  Hello Mr. Python   48
  Little Tiny Puppy Dog   31
  Malice at Buckingham Palace   24
Nash, Ogden, *Jellyfish, The*   25
  Ostrich, The   28
  Panther, The   48
Prelutsky, Jack, *Adelaide*   56
  Pigs   27
Reeves, James, *Zachary Zed*   34
Resnikoff, Alexander, *Advice*   84
  Courtship   18
  Father Goose Tells a Story   60
  Two Witches   33

Silverstein, Shel, *Do You Know the Man?*   76
    Here Are the Twins   15
    Lazy People, The   83
Smith, William Jay, *Crossing of Mary of Scotland, The*   75
Tabb, John Bannister, *Fascination*   80
Taylor, Bert Leston, *Gentle Doctor Brown*   46
West, Paul, *Cumberbunce, The*   63
Wood, Robert Williams, *Puffin, The*   44
Anonymous
    Advice to Grandsons   58
    As I Was Standing in the Street   62
    Big Rock Candy Mountain, The   87
    Boy Stood on the Burning Deck, The   54
    Deborah Delora   19
    East Is East and West Is West   86
    Framed in a First-story Winder   36
    Hannah Bantry   52
    Horses Run Around, The   78
    Johnny Went to Church One Day   72
    King Said to Salome, The   13
    Lady and the Swine, The   74
    Learner   81
    Old Joe Clarke   82
    Rhinoceroses   71
    Silly Stanzas   38
    Ten Thousand Years Ago   26
    Two Legs Behind and Two Before   45
    Two Sad Tales   14
    Who Ever Sausage a Thing?   77

TITLE INDEX

ABC, The, *Milligan*   20
Adelaide, *Prelutsky*   56
Advice, *Resnikoff*   84
Advice to Grandsons, *Anonymous*   58
As I Was Standing in the Street, *American Folk Rhyme*   62
Big Baboon, The, *Belloc*   28
Big Rock Candy Mountain, The, *American Folk Song*   87
Boy Stood on the Burning Deck, The, *American Folk Rhymes*   54
Courtship, *Resnikoff*   18
Crossing of Mary of Scotland, The, *Smith*   75
Cumberbunce, The, *West*   63
Deborah Delora, *English Folk Rhyme*   19
Dodo, The, *Belloc*   68
Do You Know the Man?, *Silverstein*   76
Dumbbell, *Cole*   59
East Is East and West Is West, *Sign in a Ceylon Zoo*   86
Fascination, *Tabb*   80
Father Goose Tells a Story, *Resnikoff*   60
Framed in a First-story Winder, *Anonymous*   36
Gentle Doctor Brown, *Taylor*   46
George, *Belloc*   40
Glue, *Burgess*   69
Hannah Bantry, *Nursery Rhyme*   52
Hello Mr. Python, *Milligan*   48
Here Are the Twins, *Silverstein*   15

Horses Run Around, The, *American Nonsense Song*   78
King Said to Salome, The, *Folk Rhyme*   13
Jellyfish, The, *Nash*   25
Johnny Went to Church One Day, *American Folk Rhymes*   72
Lady and the Swine, The, *English Folk Rhyme*   74
Lazy People, The, *Silverstein*   83
Learner, *English Children's Rhyme*   81
Little Tiny Puppy Dog, *Milligan*   31
Llyric of the Llama, A, *Johnson*   30
Malice at Buckingham Palace, *Milligan*   24
My Uncle Dan, *Hughes*   50
Old Joe Clarke, *American Folk Song*   82
Ostrich, The, *Nash*   28
Panther, The, *Nash*   48
Pigs, *Prelutsky*   27
Politeness, *Graham*   16
Puffin, The, *Wood*   44
Rhinoceroses, *Anonymous*   71
Routine, *Guiterman*   70
Sea Serpant, The, *Irwin*   22
Silly Stanzas, *American Folk Rhymes*   38
Some Sights Sometimes Seen and Seldom Seen, *Cole*   85
Ten Thousand Years Ago, *American Nonsense Song*   26
Two Legs Behind and Two Before, *Folk Rhyme*   45
Two Sad Tales, *Folk Rhyme*   14
Two Witches, *Resnikoff*   33
While Grinding Coffee at the Store, *Engel*   53
Who Ever Sausage a Thing?, *Anonymous*   77
Willie Built a Guillotine, *Engel*   43
Zachary Zed, *Reeves*   34